I0579859

Gone Astray

Three Short Stories

Purple Night

Chores Wars

Dreaming of Stars

Purple

Night

Jackie Leitch

Published by

Dayglo Books Ltd, Nottingham, UK

www.dayglobooks.co.uk

0020-15-1012-01

Cover artwork & illustrations by
www.valentineart.co.uk

Typeset in Opendyslexic
by Abelardo Gonzales (2013)

Printed by IngramSpark

Distributed by Filament Publishing Ltd, Croydon

Purple

Night

CHAPTER 1

Jojo stayed until the last seconds of the last minute. She was watching the setting suns flare in the glittering atmosphere. They cast glowing shadows across the trembling ice.

Streaks of gold, crimson and tangerine melted together with pink, pale green and deep violet.

As the last of the three suns dropped below the horizon, Jojo shook herself out of her reverie.

She had stayed longer than she had meant.

Perhaps too long. She had first felt a slow, barely

perceptible ripple in the ice. It had now become

a strong, rhythmic shudder.

She was sure she still had plenty of time to

get to the bunker. Their subterranean bolt-hole

was far below the unstable surface of the planet.

Jojo hoped it was strong enough to weather

the oncoming devastation. Everyone's lives

depended on it.

The underground station had to withstand

the enormous forces of the ice tsunami now ripping

and battering its way around the planet.

No one at Yamal Station had experienced anything like it before. But they had trained and drilled often enough for this rare event. Jojo was confident they would come through unscathed.

She hurried back to her ice-breaker. She would need to make top speed back to base. She swung herself up into the high cab.

She checked that the claws were retracted before she pressed the command for the vehicle to take off.

The ice-breaker rose several metres above the heaving ground, then sped towards safety.

CHAPTER 2

Safely back at Yamal Station, Jojo rode the pod underground. She felt breathless from the long, fast descent.

"Any word from Arktika Station?" she asked as she disembarked,

"Nothing," was the unwelcome answer.

Arktika Station was Mitch's berth. It was the first ice-mining station to be built on Planet Ice Dragon. It was located near the centre, exactly where the predicted ice tsunami was due to hit first.

Arktika Station had been out of contact since early that day.

'*Nearly 30 hours*,' Jojo thought. Her stomach knotted. If Mitch had been able to contact her, she knew he would have done so by now.

Perhaps the tsunami had already struck. Even if communications were down, the crew at Arktica should still be alive. There was emergency power, and rations enough for several weeks.

She clung to that thought. She recalled the early days of her training. The new crews had been instructed about the differences between Planet

Ice Dragon and some of the other ice planets. Her

tutor's deep, dry voice came back to her.

"On Planet Ice Dragon, each day lasts 30

hours and a year is 65 weeks. For this reason, the

Company has decided that contracts should be for

no more than three years at a time. Crews must

take at least one Earth year break before signing

on again.

"Each station is crewed by three teams. Each

team is a pair of two. Stations are single sex only.

The Company has found this to be best practice in

reducing tensions and increasing productivity."

CHAPTER 3

Jojo knew that, for most crews, a three year

stint felt like a lifetime.

Many of them resented the single sex rule.

Consequently, a significant number of men and

women did not sign on again after finishing their

initial three years.

It was an uncomfortable and tiring contract.

The stations were all deep underground. They

were small and cramped. Added to the discomfort

were the everyday problems of living in a hostile

environment and performing an incredibly

challenging job.

On top of that was the knowledge that there

was a distinct element of danger.

Planet Ice Dragon was huge. It turned slowly

in its orbit around a cluster of three dying suns.

Every so often the planet suffered massive

ice tsunamis. This was because each of the three

suns exerted its own magnetic pull. This caused

unequal stresses that triggered the ice tsunamis.

'Just our luck to be here for this one,' Jojo

thought. 'It's shaping up to be a real doozy. And we thought we'd be safe on a three year contract! What a way to earn a living – mining ice for shipment back to Earth.'

When Jojo and Mitch had signed up, three years had seemed manageable. The time and the danger were more than compensated for by the high salaries ice-miners commanded.

After all, they worked in some of the most hostile environments in the universe.

Jojo and Mitch had met during a stint on another, older planet that was nearly mined out. Mitch had been keen to try out Planet Ice Dragon.

They talked about signing up for it together

soon after they met. Their dream was to make

enough money to return home to Earth.

The pay on other planets did not compare

with the money they could make on Planet Ice

Dragon. It was a huge incentive. So, despite the

problems, they had made the decision to apply and

had both been accepted.

They calculated that their earnings, from

two three years stints, would keep them in

comfort on Earth.

Nowhere on Earth was without its problems.

Water rationing was an accepted part of life. The

imported ice that was mined off-world was

essential to keep Earth going.

But they would live in a purpose built

community in one of the last places on Earth

where it rained, so they still had natural water.

When Jojo and Mitch applied for Planet Ice

Dragon they had thought it a risk worth taking.

Given the ripples and shudders she had just

felt under her feet, Jojo was less sure now.

CHAPTER 5

"Jojo – there you are!"

Tassie, the station leader, sounded worried.

"Why did you stay out there so long? I would have

sent Sable out to look for you, but I didn't want to

risk another life."

Sable was Jojo's team pair.

Jojo apologised: "I'm sorry Tassie. I wanted

to see it as it still is, before everything changes.

I've grown to love that view and the three sunsets.

It will be very different after the ice-tsunami has

passed."

Tassie snorted.

"For Dawkins' sake, Jojo. The suns will still

be there! Honestly, who would have thought it?

You, getting sentimental about Planet Ice Dragon?

I hope it isn't catching. I don't want the rest of the

team going soft on me."

She looked closely at Jojo. "No word from

Mitch?"

Jojo grimaced. "No, not yet."

Tassie patted her hand.

"He'll be fine. They're in the deepest bunker

on the planet."

Jojo forced a smile. "Yes, I know," she said,

"I expect they're dealing with the tsunami. He'll be

in touch soon. I know he will. They're just busy."

Behind them, the chamber door opened. They

turned as Sable burst in, shouting: "Tassie! Jojo!

Come quickly! We've got a voice-link with Arktika

Station. It's really unstable. Hurry!"

They followed Sable back the way she had

come. They were desperate to get some word

about what was happening. Jojo could feel her

whole body vibrating with anxiety and tension.

Tan was on communications duty. Tan was

Tassie's team pair. Her fingers flew over the

virtual keyboard, as she fought to maintain the

fragile link.

Her clone-sisters, Alva and Oja were

standing close by. They all listened intently to the

distant voice crackling through the static.

It ebbed and flowed through the ether.

". . . damage . . . hope the airlocks . . . but . .

I can't . . ."

Jojo was frantic. It wasn't Mitch's voice. She

grabbed the coms link from Tan. "Is that you, Vic?

Where's Mitch? Can you hear me? Is Mitch okay?"

They could hear nothing. The link hissed and

buzzed intermittently. Then, faintly, the voice

again: ". . . broken . . . Mitch gone . . . just me . . ."

The women stood in silence, willing the link

to speak again. It did. ". . . so cold . . . dark . . .

need help . . ."

Then the link failed completely. Even the

static stopped.

They looked at each other. Their eyes were

wide with worry and uncertainty.

CHAPTER 6

The ice tsunami had done its worst at

Arktika Station and it was heading their way.

Arktika Station had the deepest, best

engineered bunker on Planet Ice Dragon. If Arktika

Station's bunker could not withstand the ice

tsunami, how could they hope to survive in theirs?

Jojo could hardly breathe. Had she really lost

Mitch? She had, if Vic was the only survivor. And

he would not be able to hold out if the airlocks were breached. The ice would grind its way through the bunker, crushing and destroying everything in its path.

Jojo's heart clenched at the thought that Mitch was gone. But grieving would come later. For now she needed to be strong. They all did. She breathed in deeply.

Tassie nodded at Tan, "See if you can get hold of Blue Pilot Station." Blue Pilot Station were next in the tsunami's path.

Tan called up Blue Pilot station repeatedly over the next fifteen minutes but to no avail.

Then, on Tassie's orders, she tried Krasin

Station.

"Got them!" Tan shouted. "Krasin, this is

Yamal Station. Who's that? What's happening

there?"

A clear voice responded.

"Jackson here. We're getting unbelievably

high levels of ice movement coming at us in waves.

The graph is going off the scale – and these are

just the pre-shocks. We calculate that the worst

will hit us in less than half an hour."

CHAPTER 7

Excitement or fear made Jackson's voice

sound cracked and shrill. The static on the coms

link increased.

"The ice is moving at an incredible speed. It

could be here sooner than we calculated. Our

instruments are going mad."

Tassie took the link. "Jackson," she shouted,

"you need to make yourselves safe. We think

Arktika Station has had it. The airlocks have gone."

Jackson's voice came through the buzz and crackle. "Are you sure? We did try Blue Pilot but couldn't get any response. Have you spoken to them, Tassie?"

"No. We couldn't raise them either."

The link hissed and whined. The women of Yamal Station leaned forward over the coms console, willing Jackson to respond but there was no reply.

But the connection was still open. To their dismay, the women could hear the crash of falling equipment.

And, above that noise, a deep groaning that sounded as if it was being wrenched from the bowels of the planet.

Jackson came back on. He was breathless and agitated.

"This is unbelievable. It's much, much worse than we ever dreamed it could be. The briefing information didn't describe anything like this. Our training . . . inadequate . . . deal with . . ."

The link began to stutter and break up. In the background they could hear the other men of Krasin Station yelling and orders being shouted.

They listened to the sounds of doors being

slammed shut as the men tried to engage the final

set of airlocks, before they were overwhelmed by

ice.

Tassie yelled down the link: "What's

happening? Are you okay Jackson?"

A panicked voice screamed back.

"No, no. We can't . . . . . ."

There was a shout of horror and they were

gone. The connection was dead.

CHAPTER 8

It was Jojo who said what all the other women were thinking. "It's us next."

Sable nodded. Her voice was shaking. "And it looks like we can do nothing to help ourselves. The men had practised the same drills as us. They had the same equipment and skills and experience as us. They couldn't protect themselves against the ice and neither can we."

Tan faced the other women.

"However deep the bunkers may be, the ice is crushing down deeper," she began. Runa and Oja reached for each other's hands. Tan put her arms round her two clone-sisters.

"But we're not giving up," she continued. "The three of us and the three of you are the best. We've got ourselves out of more dangerous situations than teams on any other planet. We're not beaten yet."

Tassie nodded: "We are the toughest ice-breaking team of the lot. We've mined the most and shipped the biggest loads. We won't just sit and wait, girls. We'll get out of this somehow."

Jojo nodded her agreement. There was

a chance for her and the others if they all worked

together.

Tassie turned to Sable. Sable smiled. It was

a grim, tight-lipped smile, but a smile nonetheless.

"I never doubted you all. Tan's right. We're

the best of the best. So, come on team. Let's think

of a way to beat this ice. After all, it's what we do

on a daily basis. We just have to think big, girls.

Think big. But do it fast, we don't have long."

CHAPTER 9

Tan looked around the comms room. "It's a pity we didn't get those surface screens we were promised. Without them we are blind down here."

"If it's any consolation, I don't think they would make much difference," Runa replied.

"Whichever way you cut it, it's a pretty hopeless situation."

"You know? I'm not sure I agree," Jojo said.

"We've all thought that we're safest down in the bunker. It's how we were trained. But it didn't seem to help the other teams. Maybe we would be safer outside?"

The others looked doubtful. Runa and Oja protested: "Are you kidding? We'd be shredded outside."

"Not a chance. Our best bet is to stay down here."

"I don't mean outside on the surface," Jojo explained. "I mean, get as high above the ice as we can."

"In what?" Oja looked sceptical.

"The next supply ship is not due for weeks."

"Hang on," Sable said, "Jojo might be on to something. If we suit up and get up top quickly, we can take the ice-breakers above the surface."

"I'm not sure whether we could get high enough to avoid the tsunami," Tassie argued.

"But we could try," Sable insisted. "It's better than dying down here in the dark, crushed by millions of tons of ice."

"It's a chance," Tassie agreed, "but a very small one. Those breakers aren't really designed to fly high."

CHAPTER 10

The women went back and forth over the idea. Time was fast running out for them. They knew that if they did not decide soon it would be too late.

None of them wanted to be trapped under-ground, however quick a death it might be. So, they agreed, they would do it.

If they survived, they would only have the

ice-breakers for shelter until the next supply ship

came. With the bunker wrecked there would be no

going back underground. No one voiced the

question of how they would manage then.

The odds were that they would be unlikely

to have to face that problem. They were all clear-

sighted enough to know that.

Nevertheless, they organised themselves

into collecting provisions, clothing and extra

oxygen. Within the hour, they were suited up in

their insulated, pressurised suits. They had packs

of emergency rations and medical kits ready to

load into their ice-breakers.

They always worked in teams of two, so each team took their own craft.

The women of each team hugged the others at the main door. Then they opened the airlocks.

Their first glimpse of the outside left them gaping and awestruck.

Sable gestured towards the distant horizon.

"If I wasn't so terrified, I'd think that was the most amazing sight I've ever seen."

A tumbling, screeching, wall of ice as high as a mountain was rushing towards them. It moved at a staggering speed through the purple, starlit night.

They hurried to the hangars. They tried to

run but the juddering ice beneath them made them

stumble. With every step they had to try to avoid

the sudden upheavals and factures that opened up

before their feet.

They threw their packs and themselves into

their ice-breakers. Tassie quickly gave the order to

move out.

As the cumbersome ice-breakers lifted up

from the surface, the tsunami was upon them.

CHAPTER 11

"How high is that damned thing?" Sable demanded.

"No idea," Jojo replied. She gritted her teeth as she concentrated on disabling the automatic pilot. "Not as high as we can get, I hope."

"Sable? Runa? Can you hear me?" It was Tassie on the internal coms system. Heavy static overlaid her voice.

"Yes, we hear you," Runa responded from the distance.

"But only just," Sable added.

"Okay. Last communication, last order. No heroics, let's just get ourselves out of here. We're asking a lot of these old machines. They were not built for this. So, if an ice-breaker fails, no rescue missions. Each team for itself. Okay?"

A reluctant murmur of agreement from the other five women was nearly drowned by static.

"Good luck my friends," Tassie concluded. "It's been great working with you." Then the link clicked off.

Jojo and Sable touched hands for a second.

Then Jojo completed the final disengagement of

the auto system and switched to full manual.

They were going to need all the skill and

experience they could muster to make the

attempt.

Both women broke into grim smiles. They

each used their own tried and trusted methods to

coax the heavy machine into performing a much

needed miracle.

Jojo risked a quick glance out of the side

window. She was trying to haul the ageing

ice-breaker into a climb it had never been designed

to attempt. She could see the other two vehicles

were also climbing.

37

Clanking and rattling, the three ice-breakers

drew away from the surface.

CHAPTER 12

The ice-breakers strained and fought their way through Planet Ice Dragon's atmosphere. Slowly, they inched higher and higher, as the colossal forward wave of the tsunami raced towards them.

As they gradually drew away from the surface of the planet, there were intermittent hisses and crackles from the long-range coms link.

Jojo struggled to keep a steady, upward

progress while Sable worked the com. She flicked

her fingertips over the console, trying to isolate

where the noise was coming from.

There was a sudden burst of loud static and

she thought for one mad moment that she could

hear a voice.

Sable turned towards Jojo. "Did you . . .?"

Jojo cut in. "Yes, it sounded like a voice.

But I don't think it can have been."

As she spoke a particularly violent wave of

ice passed below. The atmosphere trembled and

twisted. The ice-breaker was thrown around like

a cork on a stormy sea.

"Dawkins! That was rough." Jojo exclaimed

as she wrestled the machine back on an even keel.

Sable looked out of the lower side windows.

"Oh, Jojo," Sable moaned, "look at what's

coming."

It was the highest wall of ice so far. Its

speed defied reason. Jojo gritted her teeth and

looked at the controls.

"Yes, but we're higher. We'll make it."

She sounded determined and convinced, but

her heart was pounding against her ribs. It made

her breathless and light-headed.

'This won't do,' she thought, 'I have to get us through this. Get a grip!'

Again, she drove the ice-breaker forward and up. She used every skill she had to wrest every last drop of power out of the battered machine. She had to maintain their upward momentum against the worst the tsunami could throw at them.

She was faintly aware of a gasp from Sable, who was looking out of the window. She still had the long-range coms link open.

"There!' she shouted, "There it is again. It's definitely a voice, not static."

CHAPTER 13

For a few seconds, the voice came through clear and strong. 'Yamal Station, Yamal Station, this is Blue Pilot Station calling. Are you there?'

"Yes. Yes we are. How did you survive the tsunami?"

The voice got fainter again. The signal seemed to be drifting. Sable frantically worked the controls on the coms link.

The voice came back stronger. ". . . went up in the ice-breakers . . . tough but . . .okay." The signal was breaking up again.

Sable turned to Jojo.

"They came out like us. They used their ice-breakers and they're still alive." She was grinning madly, high on adrenalin and hope.

Jojo concentrated on keeping the craft as high as she could. The ice-breaker seemed to have a mind of its own. Without her full attention it reared up and swung from side to side.

"Yes,' she said. "I heard. Just look outside Sable. That was the biggest ice wave. The others are smaller. See, it's right below us. That's why we

lost the signal. Once it's passed, we might get Blue

Pilot back."

Jojo concentrated on holding the ice-breaker

in position above the erupting ice. Sable peered out

of the windows as a monstrous wave crushed its

way across the planet's surface below them.

"'I can't see the others, Jojo. Do you think

we've made it? Or is there worse to come?"

"I think that was the worst," Jojo sighed.

"I hope it was, because I can't get any more height.

We're up as far as we can go. And I don't know

how much longer I can hold on."

Below them, further waves of ice rolled on.

"I think the waves are getting smaller and lower," Jojo said.

They watched as the tsunami continued its terrible journey. There was no doubt, its power was diminishing with each wave that passed.

The coms link crackled into life again.

"Yamal Station, are you still there?"

Sable's voice broke as she replied.

"Yes, still here. Have you made contact with our other two teams?"

There was a pause. "No, sorry. You're the only team we've been able to reach."

Jojo and Sable looked at each other. They

had hoped to meet up with the other two teams

after the tsunami. Now, they had to accept this

would not happen.

"Yamal Station, which team are you? Your

voice sounds like Sable. Is it? And Jojo? It's hard to

tell through the static."

"Yes, Jojo and Sable. Is that Rojan? Are you

okay?" There was a pause before the answer.

"Yes, but we're the only ones who made it.

Me and my buddy Ashe. And she's hurt, but not

seriously."

Jojo and Sable felt less alone, cheered by

the sound of another human voice. Ahead, they

knew, lay a time of unimaginable difficulties until

the next supply ship arrived. There was no way to

get help any sooner. They knew it would be a long,

hard couple of weeks.

Jojo put their thoughts into words: "If we can

find a way to meet up and use the ice-breakers as

shelters, I think we might stand a chance."

Outside, the sky was getting lighter and the

planet seemed calmer.

A chance was a chance, after all. And taking

a risk had paid off once. All they could do was take

every chance to stay alive.

Chores Wars

K.M.Adlard

Published by

Dayglo Books Ltd, Nottingham, UK

www.dayglobooks.co.uk

0020-15-1012-01

Cover artwork & illustrations by
www.valentineart.co.uk

Typeset in Opendyslexic
by Abelardo Gonzales (2013)

Printed by IngramSpark

Distributed by Filament Publishing Ltd, Croydon

Chores

Wars

CHAPTER 1

"We're trying for a BABY, Stewart. Had you

forgotten?"

Jeanette's voice rises to its usual high pitch

when she has a point to make.

"I couldn't possibly entertain the idea of

a puppy!" Her voice is cutting.

"I shouldn't have a moment's peace of mind if

we had a dog AND a little one! Really, Stewart, you

don't think at all. Puppies, especially, are so

unpredictable. And messy. You'll have enough to

occupy you, I can tell you, with the cleaning and laundry and shopping and preparing meals and . . . "

Her voice trails off as she searches her mind for more chores. I notice she hasn't mentioned the garden. Need to add that to the list.

I foresaw trouble at my work soon after I took the position and long before it was announced officially in the press. The headline ran:

EXCLUSIVE —

MAJOR RETAILER CUTS TWO HUNDRED BRANCHES.

EXTENSIVE MANAGERIAL STAFF REDUNDANCIES.

'Yes, and guess who will be one of the first to go?' I said to myself, as I struggled to absorb the implications.

'Last in, first out,' my brain told me gloomily, even though I didn't want to hear it.

"A month's notice is very fair, in the circumstances, Stewart," the Area Manager informs me, with an artificial smile.

"I'm sorry to be blunt, but my main priority has to be the staff who are longer established. There will be the need for some relocation and much down-sizing, and blah blah blah blah . . ."

The Area Manager is on auto-pilot. What he really means is that he would be hanging on to the staff who were entitled to massive redundancy payments. And getting shot of newcomers like me.

Does he think I'm stupid, or what?

My wife, Jeanette, certainly thinks I am.

When I first met my wife, the characteristics which had attracted me to her had been her self-confidence and willingness to take risks. I liked

her attitude of unconcern for conventions and her

independent spirit. She was a go-getter.

Little did I realise these qualities would

backfire when I got the chop, and found myself left

in charge of the household chores.

CHAPTER 2

While I wash the dishes and do all the other domestic stuff, she trots off in her business suit at 8.15 each morning.

I suppose, in the majority of marriages, role-reversal is hell for one or the other partner. In our case it was going to be me.

Middle management is the tier most usually eliminated when a company needs to cut back. The fat cats still lazily lap their cream. The production operatives just work longer hours for less pay.

I was Mr Middle-Management personified. So, instead of getting on with my career, here I am indoors, tied into my sexy pinny and equipped with a feather duster.

"Something will soon turn up," Jeanette assures me.

"You've all that previous experience — that's what counts. And meanwhile it'll be no problem for me to work more hours. And paid maternity leave is quite generous these days. If I'm lucky enough to need it, that is."

That was thirteen months and twenty-six job applications ago.

And Jeanette is still not on maternity leave.

The way she puts on her 'ice maiden' act every time I come near her these days, the prospect is looking less and less likely.

Still, Jeanette seems happy that we're in the same situation now as a year ago.

Whilst I am not. Definitely not.

CHAPTER 3

"We've so many conveyancing contracts coming our way," Jeanette announces as she sets off for work again. "Mr Bradshaw says they could do with me in the office for some overtime. So I don't know what time I'll be home."

My first errand every day, after Jeanette leaves for the office, is to stroll to the news-agents. I buy the only paper that prints job vacancies on a daily basis.

Then back home for another, stronger, mug
of coffee and a second slice of toast with my
favourite lemon marmalade. This is the time of
day when I used to have my first smoke, as I was
approaching the office.

The fresh air rid me of the smell of
cigarette smoke, which I knew some of the girls
hated. In any case, we'd been a smoke-free area
for some time, by law.

Now I'm cash-free as well as smoke-free.
I can't afford to smoke and I shouldn't really be
having a second slice of toast, either. Ah well, I'll
take a brisk walk later. If it's not raining.

I spread the newspaper across the table
that's strewn with dirty plates and mugs. I scan
the job vacancies column. Not very long, as usual.

And the vacancies are not inspiring. But I mark
a cross with a question mark against any I feel
may be possibilities.

Then I push back my chair to get a full view
from the window. This has become my next little
routine, before I tackle clearing the table and
washing up.

"It's not worth putting those few things
through the dish washer," Jeanette has pointed
out. "It won't take you a minute or two," she tells
me, "and you've nothing more pressing to do,
have you?"

This said with a curl of the lip, and a cool
dismissiveness. Thank you, Jeanette. Little does
she know! At almost precisely this time of the
morning a certain person passes my window.

It's the young veterinary nurse who works three doors away. She's on her way to unlock the practice at the start of a new day.

At first, she didn't notice me sitting at the table by the window. Then for some reason she turned my way as she hurried along the pavement. Now, after a year, she always looks in and gives me a smile and a wave.

She's a pretty girl, with a pleasant expression. It's the sort of expression I'd welcome on Jeanette's face when she leaves in the morning or comes home at night.

Unfortunately, it's an expression I rarely see when I look at her nowadays.

'Where have things gone wrong?' I ask myself.

Is it the fact I've so far been unable to give Jeanette a child?

Is it the fact I haven't been able to secure work comparable to the job I lost?

Although it seems a ridiculous question, is it even that my standard of doing the chores isn't up to scratch?

I guess it may be a combination of all three reasons. I just know my wife rarely shows much enthusiasm for me these days.

CHAPTER 4

My wife doesn't smile at me and wave like the vet's pretty little nurse.

But this morning I seem to have missed her. Perhaps it's because I altered my morning routine a little.

I'd put washing in the machine over-night. I reasoned that as the sun was shining and the weather forecast was for showers this afternoon, I'd best hang it out quickly. I opened the washer, yanked the laundry into the basket and lugged it into the garden.

I began to hang the washing on the line. I looked at my watch and that was when disaster struck. I trailed the wet duvet cover over the lawn I mowed yesterday.

Surprise, surprise, what have appeared overnight? Nasty, moist worm casts all over the grass. I've heard the gardening experts say how beneficial worms can be. Do they tell you how messy and clingy wet worm casts are? They do not!

Blast! Blast! Blast! I bundle the duvet cover back indoors and into the washing machine again.

My little vet nurse must have passed my window long ago. Just have to wait for tomorrow.

The prospect of a whole boring day without her cheery smile to help me through it is too depressing to contemplate. I'll wash the breakfast things, then I'll have a smoke.

I can't help visualising the pert little figure, who must have passed my window while I was occupied with the washing.

On a lovely day like today, her golden pony tail would catch the sunlight as she strode along. She'd have her shoulder bag swinging with the motion of her steps.

She wouldn't be wearing a coat, so her uniform would be shown off to perfection. It's cornflower blue, which I am sure matches her eyes.

She's 'a vision of loveliness', as my dad

used to describe my mum. An old fashioned saying, I know, but it is an apt description for my little vet nurse.

In fact, I think I may have fallen for her before we've even exchanged a brief greeting. And me an old married man.

'Shame on you, Stewart,' I tell myself.

CHAPTER 5

My day improves at teatime. I answer the front door bell and who should I find standing on the step but the blue-eyed blonde in her veterinary uniform.

She smiles broadly. I'm like a love-lorn teenager. I blush as I try to return her smile.

"Hello. I'm Laura. I hope you don't mind me calling on you without warning. I don't know your name, otherwise I would have looked up your phone number."

"That's all right," I manage to mutter.

Then I notice she's carrying a fleece with something wrapped in it. The fleece moves, and a little yap escapes from under it. I can't help laughing.

Then, out pops a tousled little head, and from the other end of the fleece, a stubby little tail wagging with excitement.

"What's that?" I ask.

Laura holds up the most odd-looking little dog I've ever seen. He's a wriggling bundle of brown and grey fur with two bright eyes and a very pink tongue.

"We've got a problem at the surgery, you see," Laura explains.

"This little mite was brought in today. He

needs homing as a matter of urgency. But the dog rescue can't take him because they've got no space.

"He's so young, he ought not to be in contact with other dogs until he's had his inoculations. We've kept him in a store room all day, but there's nobody to look after him overnight."

Laura pauses for breath. Her pretty eyes gaze searchingly into mine.

"You're at home all day, aren't you?"

I nod.

"And you don't have pets, do you, or you'd have visited the surgery before now."

I nod again.

Laura takes a deep breath and plunges in.

"So we wondered if you could look after him for us until tomorrow? I know it's an awful cheek, but it really is important. I couldn't think of anyone else I could ask in an emergency. We've called him Ruff."

I reach out and smooth the puppy's furry head. He swivels round and licks my hand.

I laugh out loud. He is adorable. I lean down and murmur all sorts of silly reassuring words to him, as you do to a baby animal.

"It might have to be just temporary, I'm afraid," I tell Laura.

"That's all right. It would be wonderful if you could just help us out tonight."

"My, err, my wife is not as keen on pets as I am, you see," I explain.

I have a vibrant mental picture of what Jeanette's reaction will be. I am certain it will be the opposite of mine.

'I'll tackle that problem later,' I tell myself.

CHAPTER 6

The look of relief on Laura's face makes me feel justified in making the decision before I consult Jeanette.

"Come in," I hear myself say.

Laura steps into the hall. She holds Ruff out to me and I gently take the little chap into my arms. I can't help smiling as I try to ward off the worst of his affectionate licking of my chin and nose.

I can sense Laura's hesitation during the transfer of the puppy. Then I realise that although I've invited her into my house, I haven't introduced myself."

"I'm Stewart," I tell her. "Stewart Swift. My wife's Jeanette. She'll be home shortly."

'And then I'll be in trouble,' I add silently to myself.

"We found a little basket for Ruff," Laura is saying. "I'll just pop back to the surgery and collect it. I didn't bring it because I didn't want to seem to presume that you'd agree." She laughs as she hurries away.

A moment or two later she is back with the basket. I carry Ruff through to the kitchen and she follows.

"We do really appreciate your help," Laura assures me, as she puts the basket down. I hand Ruff back to her. She kneels down and settles him in his bed.

"What happened to him?" I ask, kneeling down by Ruff's basket and stroking him. "How did you get him?"

"It was really sad," Laura tells me. "He was being brought to us for his inoculation by his owners, who live the other side of the ring road. On the way, their car was involved in a collision. His owners both died in the accident.

"This little fellow escaped from the scene and ran away. He must have been terrified. By a miracle he made his way to this street. A kind lady found him, and she brought him to us."

"Was he hurt at all?"

"No. We've checked him over and he's fine. But the relatives of the owners say they don't want him so he's homeless."

"What a shame." I tickle Ruff behind his ears.

"Yes. And all the practice staff already have dogs of their own, so we're stuck."

Laura looks so lovely, kneeling there making a fuss of Ruff.

"Well, I'd better be going," Laura stands up. I hastily get to my feet too.

"It's quicker if you go out the back way." I open the kitchen door.

"Okay. Bye now!"

"Bye, Laura."

With that my new friend hurries away in the direction of her workplace. She turns briefly to wave to me and my new companion.

CHAPTER 7

Ruff seems entirely happy with his new surroundings. He snuffles excitedly all around the ground floor. Then he gazes longingly up the stairs. He realises they are beyond tackling on his stubby legs at present.

So he settles down in the hall, at the foot of the stairs, and goes to sleep, while I start the dinner. His coat almost matches our tweedy, oatmeal-coloured carpet.

Jeanette's voice has an irritable edge to it, before her door key is out of the lock.

"Still preparing vegetables?" is her first brusque question. "You're generally further forward than that by the time I get home!"

She bustles across the hall and almost tumbles over the sleeping Ruff.

"STEWART?" she bawls, "what's this – this CREATURE doing lurking at the foot of the stairs?"

Ruff surfaces from his nap at the sound of Jeanette's shout. He shakes himself and proceeds to fuss around her legs. He is excited, his tail wagging, his tongue hanging out.

"Get away from me, you stupid little brute," she hisses. "It was only by pure luck

I didn't fall full-length over you. Oh! What's the good of me holding a conversation with a dog!

"STEWART, how many times do I need to ask you – why is this thing in our house at all, let alone in such a stupid place? Can't you hear me, man?"

Her questions are interrupted by the back door bell. I hurry to answer it, and there is Laura.

"I forgot to give you Ruff's bowl," she says, smiling. "And some food for him. I'm so sorry."

I take the bowl and the bag of dog food from her and smile back. "Thank you."

'Hell, what timing,' I think to myself, but it can't be helped. It's not Laura's fault my wife's such a short-tempered witch.

By this time Jeanette has perched herself on one of the high stools at the breakfast bar. I'm sure it is to put herself in a superior position to me.

"Well?" she repeats.

"Well, what?"

"I think I'm entitled to an explanation Stewart, don't you? As to why an attractive young blonde is visiting you via our back door. AND, once again, why this animal has made itself at home in our house?"

Jeanette scowls, as only she can.

"Is there any real rush about this," I ask as I put out dog food and set Ruff's bowl down for him by the fridge. "Can't I just complete the meal preparation and then we can sit down calmly to discuss the matter?"

"Real rush?'" Jeanette explodes. "There most certainly is a real rush. And no way would I consider sitting down to a meal in the same room, even in the same house, as this . . . this . . .."

Jeanette's voice trails off again. She seems incapable of finding a word damning enough to describe Ruff.

I realise I will have to come clean to her about my plans to keep Ruff. But at least I can sit on the other high stool and tackle the matter, literally, face to face.

I feel a stiff drink might help my confidence, but decide I must just press on without one.

CHAPTER 8

"The little puppy is homeless and too young to be put in a kennel with other dogs," I explain. "I've told the young lady from the vet's that it's only on a temporary basis. After all, Jeanette, the house is in joint ownership and I do spend an awful lot of time in it these days so I reckon I can do as I like in it."

This is obviously not a good line to adopt in my present financial situation. Jeanette jumps at her opportunity almost before the words are out of my mouth.

"Joint ownership, Stewart? Do you realise you're speaking to someone who may be your wife, but is also knowledgeable about these matters through her work. And who, as you very well know, has been making the mortgage repayments on our 'jointly owned' house for well over a year – while you swan around here doing very little except ask for more money to foot the household bills."

The sneer in her tone is very obvious as she clambers back off the stool, retrieves her shoes, coat and handbag and delivers her parting shot.

"Don't bother to continue preparing supper on my behalf, Stewart. I shall eat out. I'll phone you about nine and if this creature has not been accommodated somewhere other than our 'jointly owned property', I shall make other sleeping arrangements also."

With that, she flounces out of the front door, slamming it behind her as hard as she can.

I shrug towards Ruff's enquiring face.

"Didn't expect her to take quite such a firm line, old fellow," I assure him. "Never mind. We have each other, don't we? She'll soon come round when she realises what hotel bed and breakfast charges are."

Ruff wags his tail in agreement and trots pointedly towards his food bowl as if to say: 'Yeah, and I don't think much of the service in this hotel up to now!' I give him a refill.

As good as her word, the phone rings at nine o'clock on the dot. I know it will be Jeanette.

"Well?" she barks down the line. "Have you made other arrangements?"

"No, Jeanette, I haven't. And I think your attitude is totally unreasonable, considering how little time you spend at home these days, and how long I'm here on my own, through no fault of mine."

There is a pause while I sense she mulls over my reply. Then, obviously keeping tight control on her voice, Jeanette continues:

"In that case I'd like you to walk round to the Imperial hotel."

Before I can ask why, Jeanette continues:

"That's where I'm phoning from. I'm with someone I think you should meet. We're in the main lounge, near the window."

And without further explanation Jeanette cuts off the call.

I am left, as always, with no option but to comply with her demand.

CHAPTER 9

A tall, distinguished looking man rises from his seat beside Jeanette as I enter the hotel lounge. He beckons me over. Jeanette introduces him.

"This is Mr Bradshaw, Stewart. Henry Bradshaw, my employer and something more than that, in case you hadn't suspected . . ."

Her voice tails off in anticipation of some reply from me.

'But what reply?' I ask myself, 'Pleased to meet you. Can I get you both a drink? Nice hotel, I've not been here before.'?

Or just the bald question: 'What the hell do you mean by that remark, Jeanette?'

In the end I just seat myself at the other side of the low table and say nothing. I wish I had thought to buy myself a drink before I joined them.

Jeanette does not wait long to continue her explanation. Her lips are a tight line, but she does have the grace to blush as she blurts out:

"As you know, I've been working full time for over a year now. I had been planning to have a frank talk with you in the comfort of our own home. However, as that's not possible, I won't beat about the bush any longer."

She hesitates. It seems to me she is deliberately playing for time as she reaches for her glass and takes a drink.

"For some time," she continues, "Henry and I have been lovers as well as work colleagues."

All I can do is a splutter at this piece of news.

She sees the look on my face and takes another sip of her tonic water. Then she speaks again.

'*There is more?*' I think.

"And, and . . . I'm expecting Henry's baby in about six months' time."

She brushes an imaginary crumb or piece of fluff from her immaculate skirt, to avoid my eyes. Henry grasps her hand protectively.

I am at a total loss for words.

'*I must appear a complete idiot in front of this suave boss-cum-lover,*' I think.

I say nothing. Henry seems to feel obliged to contribute to the conversation, so he adds:

"Sorry this seems to come as a complete surprise to you, Stewart. I would have thought you might have had some doubts as to the likelihood of Jeanette working such excessive hours.

"However, be sure that now it's all out in the open, I shall do the right thing by Jeanette, of course. I've quite a sizeable residence in the best part of town. If solicitors can't attract a good income then who can, eh?"

He squeezes my wife's hand as he smirks at his own joke.

'Pity the poor bloke who can not only earn nothing at present, but who can't even father his own child,' I think to myself.

I realise nothing can be achieved at that time of night, particularly in a hotel lounge. I stand up quickly and turn away from the pair.

Far be it from me to enquire where my wife will be spending the night.

"Let me know when you want to come round for your things, Jeanette," I mutter, and leave.

The enthusiasm with which Ruff greets me on my return is heartening. I bury my crumpled face in his shock of fur.

"Come on, old chap," I encourage him, "we can do as we like in future. Fancy sharing my bed, since she doesn't want to?"

The alarm clock and Ruff scrabbling frantically at the back door wake me in good time next day. I am surprised at how good I feel this morning.

After breakfast, I gather Ruff into my arms and we wait at the front gate for a 'vision of loveliness' to happen along.

Dreaming

of

Stars

Jackie Leitch

Published by

Dayglo Books Ltd, Nottingham, UK

www.dayglobooks.co.uk

0020-15-1012-01

Cover artwork & illustrations by
www.valentineart.co.uk

Typeset in Opendyslexic
by Abelardo Gonzales (2013)

Printed by IngramSpark

Distributed by Filament Publishing Ltd, Croydon

Dreaming

of

Stars

CHAPTER 1

The sand is both soft and hard. It is soft in my fingers as I run them through the grains, hard beneath my body. I lie straight, with my arms out-stretched. It's about 4 a.m. and I am very drunk.

There are no street lamps in this small remote costal town in Western Australia, therefore no light pollution. Just a rich blue-black sky alive with brilliant starlight and the perfect sphere of the moon casting soft pale shadows.

Tentatively, I open my eyes again. This time, the stars and the moon do not dance around like whirling dervishes. 'Maybe I'm sobering up,' I think.

I have never seen so many stars before. The Southern Hemisphere has far more stars than the cold grey-black night sky in my Northern European home.

The sheer beauty – and possibly the alcohol – bring tears to my eyes. The still figure beside me stirs. I thought he was sleeping but, no, he too is awake and enjoying the light show.

Neither of us speaks. The moment is too precious for words. He takes my hand in his and loosely links our fingers. We could be alone in the world.

The absence of sound or street lights or people confers a kind of freedom to be no more than we are at that moment – two human beings, side by side on the shore of a land more ancient than any other.

Donny gives a faint grunt as he untangles our fingers and sits up. "Sleepy. Gotta go to bed." he mumbles. He plants a soft kiss on my cheek and stands up. Momentarily, he blocks out the moon. Staggering slightly, he leaves me alone in the night.

I do not reply or acknowledge him in any way. I am too caught up in the shimmer and glitter of the night and the whoosh of alcohol through my blood. At last, even I tire of the beauty. I've looked so long the spectacle has become commonplace.

The wooden cabin we are staying in is only a short stumble from the beach. Donny is deep in sleep as I strip off my shorts and T-shirt and fall into bed.

At first, I find it hard to drift off. The bed seems unstable, liable to veer one way or the other. A few times I find myself clutching at the edge of the mattress, fearful that I might fall out.

When, finally, sleep overcomes me, it is disturbed by jumbled dreams and fearful encounters. When I wake fitfully, the hot little cabin feels claustrophobic and sweaty.

The air is pressing in on me. Irritated, I throw off the tangled covers and slide away into dreams again.

CHAPTER 2

Donny has gone for his usual swim by the time I wake up. I straighten the bed-covers and pick up a lone feather from the floor.

"Only two more days here at Coral Bay," I think, "then it's time to move on."

Without thinking, I push the feather into the pocket of my shorts. Then I start to make a simple breakfast of fruit, pancakes and coffee.

I glance at my watch and wonder where Donny has got to. "*Lost track of the time,*" I tell myself. "*Nothing to worry about.*"

Minutes pass, then half an hour has gone by. I go to the door. The German couple from two cabins down are walking back from the beach, hand in hand.

"Hi", I call, "Did you see Donny around?" I try not to sound over-anxious.

"No, Grace." Axel replies and Kristin shakes her head too. "We are all alone on the beach. No one else is there."

"OK, thanks."

I try to sound casual, as if it was just a passing comment.

They step up onto the decking and come over to the door.

"Are you worrying, Grace?" Kristin asks, with a frown of concern. Axel puts a hand each side of the door-frame and leans in, the sunshine high-lighting the red-gold of his stubble.

"You need some help maybe?" he offers. Obviously, I had not sounded as casual as I had thought.

"No, not really." I deny. Then my fear spills out, panicky words stumbling one over another. "Only, he doesn't usually swim for longer than half an hour, and . . . and he was already gone when I woke up more than an hour ago."

My voice sounds strange to me, more sob

than speech, choked and yet shrill. By now, I am making no attempt to sound unconcerned.

Putting my worries into words has made them more real. I can feel myself verging on hysteria. My heart pounds and my legs go weak and shaky. Kristin puts out her hand, runs it gently along my arm:

"Come then, Grace, we will look together for Donny." Axel nods his agreement. The three of us walk back to the beach in the hot, still air.

The small office out of which the lone policeman operates is blessedly air-conditioned. Even so, I can feel myself sweating with apprehension.

Sergeant Campbell writes down everything

I tell him in my anxious, wobbly voice. He asks questions I cannot answer.

"So, do you have any idea what time he went off for his swim?", and, "Did he always go at the same time?", and, "You say you didn't hear him go?"

All these questions – until my story begins to sound odd and disjointed. I feel disconnected from the events of the morning, as if it is happening to someone else.

The questions are unbearable to me. I wish he would just stop querying everything I say and go look for Donny.

CHAPTER 3

Axel and Kristin take their turn to tell the policeman what they know. They have little to add to my story. After all, they only came onto the scene after Donny had already gone.

They are keen to be helpful, but they really have nothing to say. The Sergeant is kind: "Don't worry Ms Jackson, we'll take a gander round. He's probably gone off for some more bread or beer and forgotten how long he's been gone."

I try to smile but my heart is beating hard in my throat. I cannot concentrate on making my muscles form a smile, not even a small one.

I stop off to see Ray, the owner of the half-a-dozen cabins on the site. I explain what happened. Tell him about the visit to the police and my fears for Donny.

He is sympathetic but unconcerned. He puts an arm round my shoulder, tries to reassure me:

"No worries, sweetheart. Stay as long as you like. I'll bet ya Donny will be back before ya know it. And Mac's a decent bloke, he'll see ya right."

"Who's Mac?" I wonder. Then I realise it is Sergeant Campbell.

CHAPTER 4

The cabin provides no respite from the thoughts running through my mind. So many questions.

Later, the Sergeant comes to find me again. He says I must go to the station to give a formal statement and sign it.

The atmosphere in the small office is less relaxed and more unreal even than before. Axel and Kristin have been asked to return, too.

The Sergeant drops us off at the cabins. He says he wants a word with Ray anyway, so it is no problem to give us a lift.

"What kind of a word does he want with Ray?" I wonder.

Answering my own question, I realise he will want to ask about Donny and I. He will want to know how we seem together. To see if Ray had heard any raised voices, or arguments.

In short, he is looking for anything to suggest we are not the loving couple we appear to be at first sight.

CHAPTER 5

The following day the Sergeant comes for me again. I am to be questioned further about what I remember.

"Just to get everything clear in our own minds," the Sergeant explains.

"*It seemed to me that it was perfectly clear the first time I said it,*" I thought.

We go over it all again.

He asks. I answer. I feel close to tears.

"What more can I say?" I ask him, "I've told you everything I know."

Disturbed nights and exhaustion take their toll. My dreams are troubling. Most nights they are filled with bewildering images.

Not only am I grief stricken, to add to my woes I feel I am becoming paranoid.

Axel and Kristin try to be positive and supportive. Their kindness gets on my nerves after a while. What I want is to be left alone.

No more questions. No more 'talking it over', whatever that means. What I need is Donny back with me, loving me, calming me.

Sometimes, my fear turns to anger. I stalk about the cabin, muttering out loud.

I tell Donny how furious I am with him for just going off like that. What was he thinking, leaving me alone and vulnerable in a strange country?

In my mind, I shout at him. I give him a good telling off. I make him understand how frightened he has made me.

The anger does not last. I go down to the shore and walk along the waterline, crying and pleading with Donny to return to me.

CHAPTER 6

Donny is nowhere to be found.

Belatedly, the police Sergeant searches our
cabin. He carefully goes through Donny's things. He
rifles through the paperback Donny was reading.
He takes his time feeling through Donny's clothes.

Then he examines the bed and bedding. He
takes everything out of Donny's wallet. He looks
at the credit cards, some receipts, his U.K. driving
licence.

There is nothing of any significance. Nothing to cause a man to disappear.

Now, the Sergeant turns his attention to our travel documents, our suitcases, my clothes. We do not have much with us, so he is soon done with our belongings. He opens the cupboards and drawers, looks at the knives.

"Were there any tools in the cabin?"

I give a small shrug and shake my head, not sure what he is after.

"You know, wrenches or spanners, screwdrivers, that sort of thing? Maybe a shovel?"

"No." I say.

Next, he searches our hired car, pulls out the spare tire, examines the jack.

Later, he returns with two more men. They poke and prod with long poles along the seashore above the high water mark. They push the poles into the dense sand and then into the soft thin soil the cabin stands on.

When they are done, he tells me to stay in Coral Bay for now.

"Until we see where we are . . ." He trails off, appearing uncomfortable and ill-at-ease with what he has to say.

"*I know where I am,*" I think, "*I'm in Coral Bay without Donny.*"

CHAPTER 7

I wonder where the Sergeant is going with his thinking. Despite the heat, I feel chilled.

"Do you think I killed him?" I ask. My voice is squeaky and shaky. I sound guilty even to myself.

"No, it's just procedure, Ms Jackson. Just routine." he assures me. I am not convinced. I know he thinks that Donny is dead and I am responsible.

The police check hospitals all along the

coast. The hospitals are few and far between.
They put out alerts. They request the public to
report any sightings. They issue a description:

'White male, 5'7" tall, small boned and of
slim build. Aged 32. Hair: mid length, blond and
curly, with a close trimmed blond beard and grey
eyes. Speaks with an English accent. Last seen
wearing navy shorts and a red T-shirt with
a Foster's beer logo on the front.'

"Last seen naked in bed," I think.

I am kept waiting nearly three weeks.
Sergeant Campbell, or Mac, as I am now to call him,
comes to the cabin to see me.

"I thought I'd better let you know the state
of play." he says.

He sits on the bed, his crumpled uniform tight and sweaty under his arms.

"Basically, we have no more idea of where your partner is or what's happened to him than we did three weeks ago. I'm sorry, Grace, we're just nowhere on this."

I make no response. What is there to say?

I feel he expects some comment but I can think of nothing to say to help him, or myself.

The expectant expression on his face is replaced by his usual genial half-smile. He rubs the sweat off his forehead. He stands up and squashes his hat back on his head.

It is the news I have been expecting, yet I feel hollowed out by the bald statement.

Mac is speaking again. I try to concentrate.

"You can go back to the U.K. whenever you want. I'll keep in touch. Let you know if anything turns up."

"Like Donny's body," I think.

"I'll keep looking, I promise." Mac comes towards me. For a moment it seems as though he is going to embrace me but instead he shakes hands rather formally. I would have preferred a hug but he is not really a friend, just a kind policeman.

CHAPTER 8

The flight home has the dream-like quality of a half-forgotten film. The bland smiles of the check-in staff seem hostile and robotic. The cabin crew appear friendly but I feel their looks as accusations.

They offer me a whole three-seater row to myself. I wonder if they think that I might contaminate my fellow travellers. Nevertheless, I accept.

'*I'm sure they mean to be kind,*' I tell myself, but I am not really sure of anything.

Somehow, I am home, standing in my hallway. I have little recollection of the flight, of claiming my bags at the airport, or the taxi ride back to our flat.

I suppose my family and friends will rush round with offers of help. The door-bell will ring, my mobile will buzz.

People will insist that I need company and support. They will sit and sympathise and then offer me clichés and well-meaning advice. I shall be encouraged to adjust, get on with my life, put it all behind me.

'How should I do that?' I wonder. 'How does anyone do that?'

I throw the dirty washing into the laundry bin. The feather I found in the cabin the day Donny went missing is still in my shorts pocket. I tuck the feather in between the pages about Coral Bay in my 'Lonely Planet' guide book. I put the book on the shelf in our bedroom. I know I shall never return to Australia.

All the other bits and pieces we had collected were left behind when I packed up to come home. A few pale pink shells. The dried starfish. A couple of odd shaped stones. It was not much but, by then, I no longer wanted to bring home these souvenirs of the perfect trip.

For the first few months, I hear regularly from Mac, the Sergeant at Coral Bay. He e-mails me with news of possible new leads.

He tells me of people he has spoken to such as boat-owners, hospital staff, haulage businesses, delivery drivers. He reassures me that he will not give up.

Gradually, though, the e-mails become less regular and less frequent. Then, Mac e-mails the news that he is moving stations.

The new guy contacts me but he holds out no hope. He says Mac had covered everything possible and there is nothing more he can do. He has no new leads. There is no-one left to speak to.

He expresses the opinion that it is

a complete mystery. They will keep the case open

but I should not expect any new developments for

the foreseeable future.

When Mac goes I lose my last connection to

Coral Bay.

Axel and Kristin returned to Germany

a month or so after I left. Kristin wrote, saying

that the place had lost its 'spiritual essence' – her

words. I do not hear from them again.

CHAPTER 9

I try to reconcile myself to the idea that I will never see Donny again. Nor will I ever know what happened to him on that hot, early morning swim.

As in the past, the stress of being alone, and not knowing what happened to Donny, brings on nightmares. That, and the drinking.

Alone in the flat, I reach too often for the wine. I drink myself into a stupor.

It is a state that, for a while, passes for sleep.

Time after time, I go back to that starlit night, Donny warm beside me on the sand.

I recall the short stagger to the hot cabin and awaking to an empty bed the next morning. How did everything go so wrong?

Sometimes, in an attempt to console myself, I lie in bed creating alternative scenarios.

Donny went out again during the night for a late swim while still drunk. He got into trouble and drowned. "So, why didn't his body wash up?" I ask myself.

"Could a shark have eaten him?" Repulsed by the thought, I push away the image of Donny, torn and bleeding, in the saw-toothed mouth of a large white shark.

No, a better picture is of Donny going for his usual early morning swim. He swims out a bit too far, gets caught up in a strong current and gets washed away.

I imagine a kindly couple in a smart, modern boat. They see him in the water and fish him out. He is half-dead with exhaustion and near drowned. Traumatised, he is suffering from amnesia. They take him to a hospital hundreds of miles away in the direction they were sailing. Donny never regains his memory of who he is, or of me.

Although it saddens me, this is a scenario I can live with.

CHAPTER 10

The night terrors, which have plagued me on

and off all my life, return frequently to disturb my

sleep. I resolve to give up alcohol, which has

always made them much worse.

With no Donny here to soothe and comfort

me, my nights are often fraught and violent.

I seem to startle awake.

Somehow, I am back in the cabin with the

moonlight casting pale, ghostly shadows across

a twisted, humped form. The air seethes. A dark shape touches and pulls me. Its face is ugly, the mouth open ready to tear my flesh.

I feel evil all around me. It is in the very air that I am gasping at, trying to suck into my lungs.

I fight back as best I can but the creature turns and writhes under me. It is strong, so strong. But in the end I am stronger. Fear and horror drive me on to defeat it.

At last, I am able to push a pillow over its twisted face. Until then, I am not sure that I can beat it. The terrible thrashing of its limbs finally stops. There is a hard pounding in my head and I am slick with sweat and fear.

A heartbeat later, and I am standing on the

shore, watching the sea slide lazily back and forth across the sand. The water is starlit, in phosphorescent shades of vivid blue and green.

I swim through the warm caressing ocean, dragging the dead beast with me. I swim out past the fringe of coral reef which lies close to the shore.

I cast the evil into the depths beyond for the sharks to deal with. And, at last, I feel safe and I can sleep again.

I awake from these vivid horrors with an angry thundering in my head and my heart full of terror. After such hellish dreams, I keep the light on for the rest of the night, to dispel the tormenting shadows.

CHAPTER 11

Today is the second anniversary of the day Donny was lost to me. I still hurt with missing him. The pain never seems any less.

Thankfully, the night horrors are not the only dreams I have. Every so often, in the cool, dark English nights, I sleep sweetly.

On those nights I dream of Coral Bay as I want to remember it. The stars are glittering and glimmering like brilliant cut diamonds.

The opalescent moon casts a pale, shimmering light.

Donny lies on the beach beside me again, warm in the night, his fingers loosely entwined with mine.

The sand is both soft and hard beneath me.